Why the Crab Has No Head

an African tale retold and illustrated
by Barbara Knutson

 Carolrhoda Books, Inc./Minneapolis

The name *Nzambi Mpungu*
is pronounced
n'ZAHM-bee m'POON-goo.

LIBRARY OF CONGRESS CATALOGING-IN-PUBLICATION DATA

Knutson, Barbara.
  Why the crab has no head.

  Summary: Retells the African folktale from the
Bakongo people of Zaire in which Crab's pride influences
his creator, who leaves Crab without a head to make him
humble.
  [1. Folklore–Zaire. 2. Crabs–Folklore] I. Title.
PZ8.1.K728Wh   1987   [E]   87-18278
ISBN 0-87614-322-2 (lib. bdg.)

Manufactured in the United States of America

1 2 3 4 5 6 7 8 9 10 97 96 95 94 93 92 91 90 89 88 87

With awe and thanks to
the African tale-spinners,
who have been telling
new and old stories for centuries

It was Nzambi Mpungu who made the earth and the sky.

And after that, my children, she made the Guineafowl and the Crocodile, the Turtle and the Gazelle. She made the Leopard and the Lizard.

And still she was not finished.

She took one whole day
to make the Elephant,
and that was heavy work.

The sun was setting that same day when Nzambi began on yet another animal.

"I will call this little one Crab," she decided, shaping a tough shell for the body and for each many-jointed leg. She made not just two legs, or four, but eight of them. Ai, but she was tired by the time she finished the last leg!

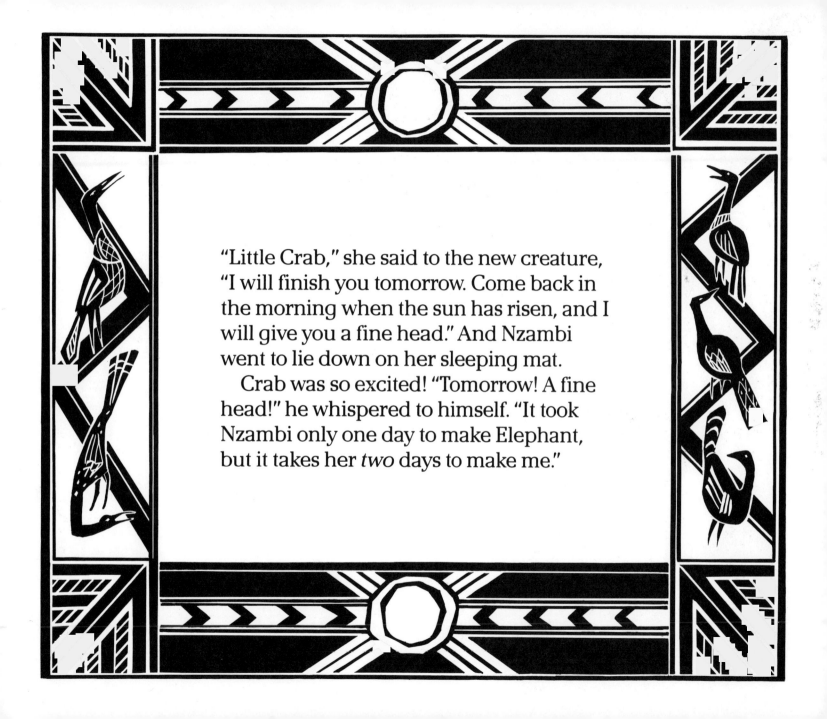

"Little Crab," she said to the new creature, "I will finish you tomorrow. Come back in the morning when the sun has risen, and I will give you a fine head." And Nzambi went to lie down on her sleeping mat.

Crab was so excited! "Tomorrow! A fine head!" he whispered to himself. "It took Nzambi only one day to make Elephant, but it takes her *two* days to make me."

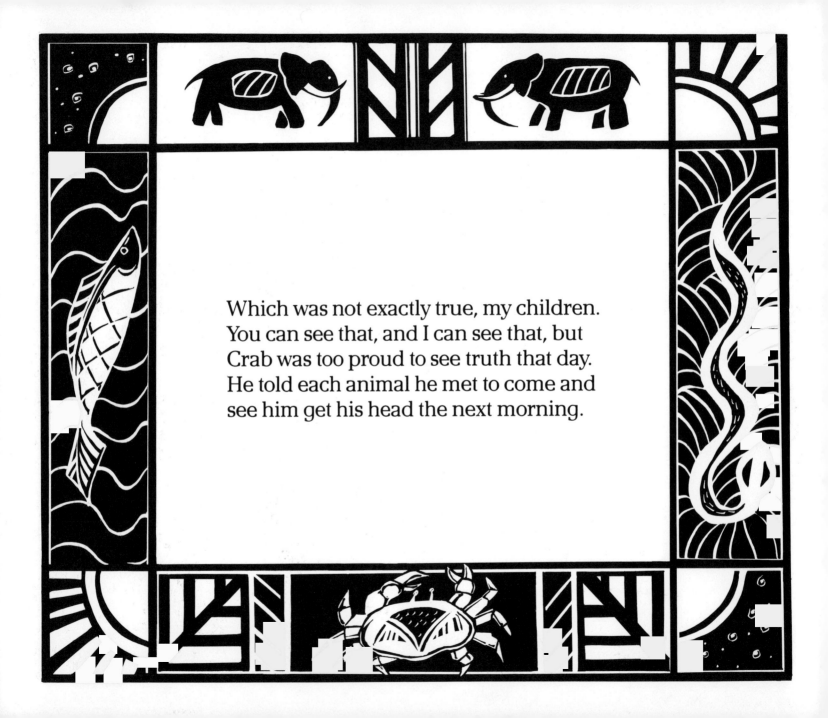

Which was not exactly true, my children.
You can see that, and I can see that, but
Crab was too proud to see truth that day.
He told each animal he met to come and
see him get his head the next morning.

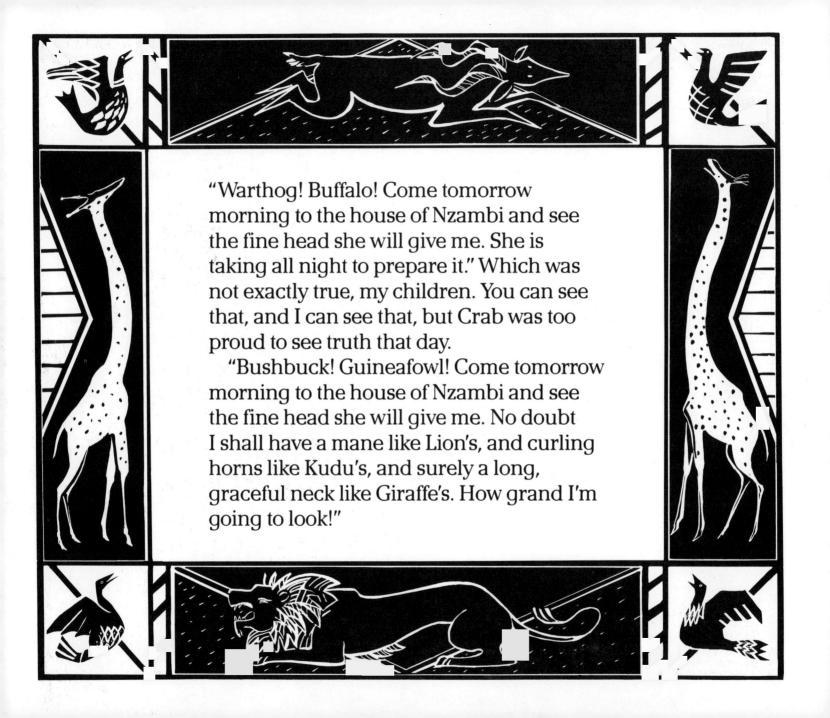

"Warthog! Buffalo! Come tomorrow morning to the house of Nzambi and see the fine head she will give me. She is taking all night to prepare it." Which was not exactly true, my children. You can see that, and I can see that, but Crab was too proud to see truth that day.

"Bushbuck! Guineafowl! Come tomorrow morning to the house of Nzambi and see the fine head she will give me. No doubt I shall have a mane like Lion's, and curling horns like Kudu's, and surely a long, graceful neck like Giraffe's. How grand I'm going to look!"

He scurried away importantly,
walking almost sideways with pride.

The next morning
at sunrise, there was
a great crowd at the
house of Nzambi.

The whole Impala family was there because they were always very curious. The Monkeys came ready to laugh at Crab, no matter how grand he was going to look. Lion came because he had heard that Crab dared to compare his new head to Lion's own magnificent head. Vulture showed up in case there might be food, and the Lizards arrived when the sun was warm on the walls where they liked to bask.

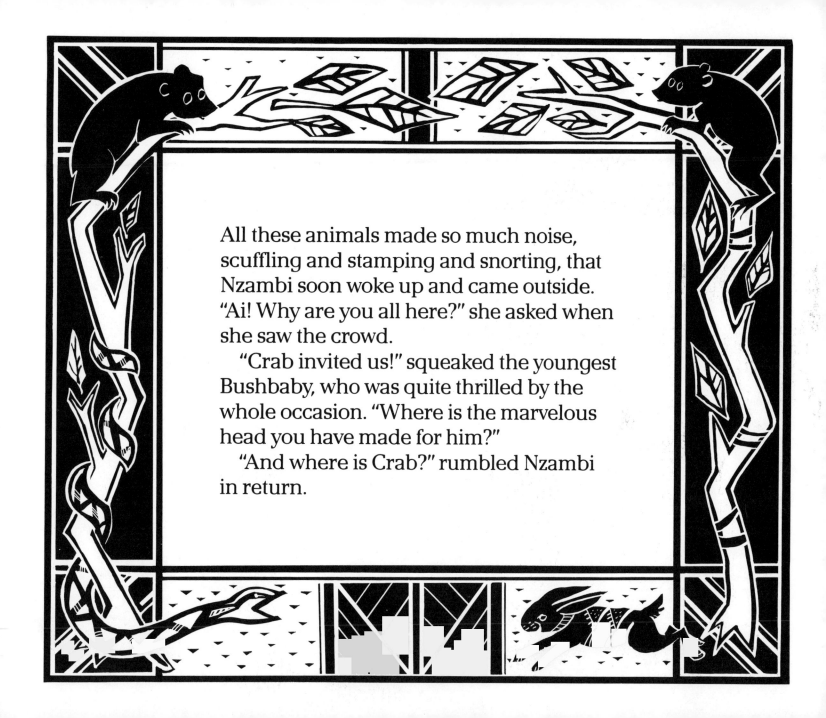

All these animals made so much noise, scuffling and stamping and snorting, that Nzambi soon woke up and came outside. "Ai! Why are you all here?" she asked when she saw the crowd.

"Crab invited us!" squeaked the youngest Bushbaby, who was quite thrilled by the whole occasion. "Where is the marvelous head you have made for him?"

"And where is Crab?" rumbled Nzambi in return.

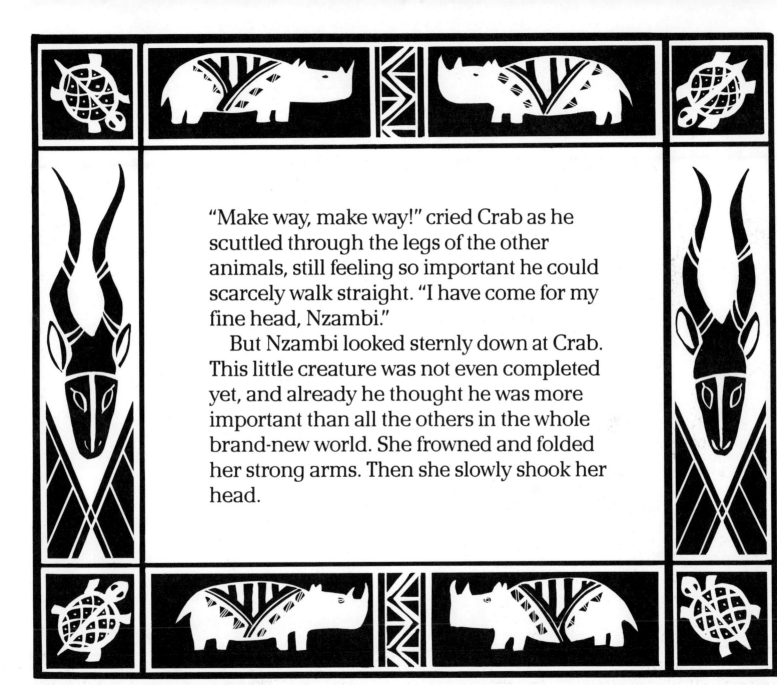

"Make way, make way!" cried Crab as he scuttled through the legs of the other animals, still feeling so important he could scarcely walk straight. "I have come for my fine head, Nzambi."

But Nzambi looked sternly down at Crab. This little creature was not even completed yet, and already he thought he was more important than all the others in the whole brand-new world. She frowned and folded her strong arms. Then she slowly shook her head.

"No, Crab," said Nzambi at last. "I think you are fine just the way you are." Now *that* was perfectly true, my children. And Nzambi went back into her hut to think about how many stripes she wanted to put on the Zebra she would make that day.

So Crab never did get a head. To this day, whenever he wants to see he has to poke his eyes out from his body.

And he still walks sideways, only now it is from embarrassment instead of pride.